This book belongs to:

....

....

For Matilda Sue

A TEMPLAR BOOK

First published in the UK in 2023 by Templar Books,
an imprint of Bonnier Books UK
4th Floor, Victoria House,
Bloomsbury Square, London WC1B 4DA
Owned by Bonnier Books
Sveavägen 56, Stockholm, Sweden
www.bonnierbooks.co.uk

1 3 5 7 9 10 8 6 4 2

ISBN 978-1-80078-621-9

This book was typeset in Clarendon
The illustrations were created digitally

Edited by Alison Ritchie
Designed by Genevieve Webster
Production by Nick Read

Printed in China

templar
books

A BAD DAY FOR BEAR

DUNCAN BEEDIE

Bear strode out of his cave and felt the warm sun
on his face. He was in a good mood.

Tonight it was the forest party. All his friends
were coming and he had a very important job to do.
He was in charge of building the bonfire!

First he set off to collect some wood.

He found a big stick that looked perfect,
but when he picked it up . . .

He got a splinter in his paw.

It hurt **a lot.**

The ladybirds heard Bear's cries.

"Ouch, that looks sore," said Daddy Ladybird.

"You need to find some wood that isn't so splintery."

Bear headed off to find some better wood.

I'm sure there'll be some in the forest, he thought, when suddenly . . .

C-R-A-A-C-C-K!

A falling log
whacked Bear
on the head.

"**Ouch!** Today was meant to be a good day," he whimpered. "But so far I've got a splinter and a big bump on my head."

"Sorry about that," chattered Beaver, "I've been chopping down trees for my dam. Here, take some of this wood for the campfire."

"Thanks, Beaver," Bear said, rubbing his head.

As Bear began dragging the logs, it started to rain.

"Oh dear!" he sighed. "I've got
a splinter in my paw, a big bump
on my head **and** now all the firewood
is soaking wet too. Today really
is the worst day **ever**!"

Then Bear had an idea. He would go and visit
his wise friend, Frog. Frog always knew
how to make everything better.

He was lugging the wood towards
the pond, when . . .

. . . he tumbled into an enormous muddy puddle and
got covered in thick, gloopy mud from nose to tail.
"G-R-R-R-A-A-R-R-G-H!" he wailed.

Bear **was** having a **bad** day . . .

A very bad day . . .

indeed.

"Dearie me," gasped Frog,
  as he spotted Bear trudging over.
  "What's happened to you?"

"Oh Frog! I'm having a **very bad** day!" sniffled Bear.
"I've been trying to collect wood for the campfire and
so far, I've got a splinter in my paw . . .
a **big** bump on my head . . . soaking wet logs –
and **now** I'm all covered in mud!"

Bear **burst** into tears.

"Don't worry, Bear,"
soothed Frog. "Let's start
with the first problem."

Frog inspected Bear's paw with his **big**, goggly eyes.

He plucked the splinter out.

"There!" Frog said. "Take a look at the thing that was causing you all that bother. It's actually teeny tiny."

Bear studied the splinter – it was indeed teeny tiny.

"But what about the **big** bump on my head?" he moaned.

Frog felt Bear's head.

"It's actually rather a small bump," he said.

Bear felt the bump. It did feel quite
small now. *It must have shrunk,*
he thought.

"And now that the sun's come out, even that great big puddle you fell in isn't so big," chimed Frog.

"Sometimes we can turn the smallest things into big problems. But when you take time to look at them, they're not really big problems at all."

"I expect your logs have dried out now too," Frog added.

"But so has the mud on my fur!" groaned Bear. "How will
  I get it all off?"

"I can think of one way . . . " smiled Frog.

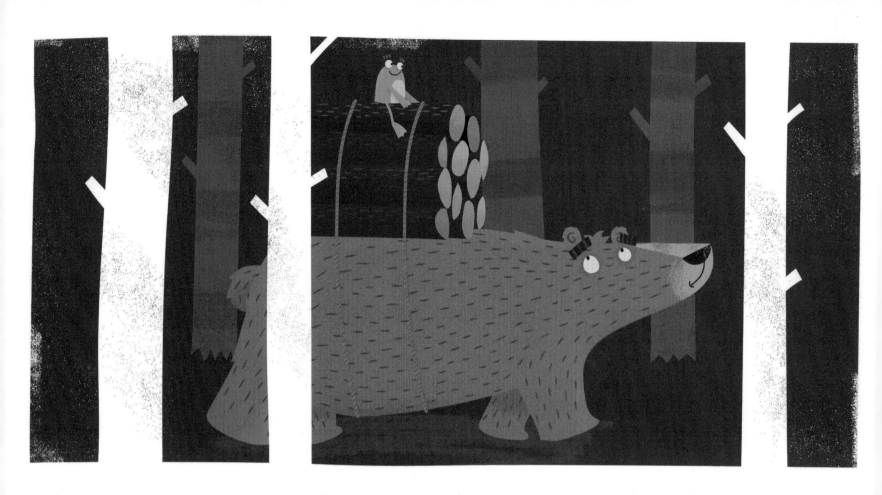

When all the mud was gone, they carried the logs to the clearing.

Frog helped Bear with his very important job.

Soon the campfire was lit and the party was in full swing.

As darkness fell, Bear and his friends toasted marshmallows in the warm glow of the fire. They ate until their tummies were full.

"Oh drat!" barked Badger, when the fire started to go out.
"It's gone **all** dark."

"That's not a problem," answered Bear. "Look up . . .

. . . now you can see the beautiful night sky!"

Bear and his friends lay back and gazed at the glittering stars.

"You know what, Frog?" Bear said, licking his marshmallowy lips.

"Today hasn't been such a bad day after all."

THE END